Maya & Miguel

FAMILY FIX-UP

Adapted by C. Tobin
Art Direction by Rick DeMonico
Designed by Heather Barber

ISBN 0-439-69606-2

12 11 10 9 8 7 6 5 4 3 2   5 6 7 8 9/0

Printed in the U.S.A.
First printing, April 2005

SCHOLASTIC INC.

NEW YORK   TORONTO   LONDON   AUCKLAND   SYDNEY
MEXICO CITY   NEW DELHI   HONG KONG   BUENOS AIRES

Like the time she decided that math lessons in school were getting too boring...
Or the time she decided that having a convertible would make our Papi feel young again...
Too bad it rained.
Anyway, this story is about the time Maya decided to play matchmaker...

IN THE SANTOS FAMILY'S APARTMENT, MIGUEL AND TITO PLAYED HIDE-AND-SEEK BEFORE SUNDAY DINNER WAS SERVED . . .
¡AY!
YES!
Nobody tell Miguel where I'm hiding.

SCREECH!

Oh, no. Maya, I know that look. So whatever plan you're cooking up...don't.

I must.
Try. *Please?*
It's too important. Miguel, look around the room. Do you notice something horribly wrong?
Yeah, I'm standing here talking to you instead of playing hide-and-seek with Tito.

All the adults have someone special except Abuelita. Papi has Mamá and Tío Ernesto has Tía Teresa.
So?
So? Can't you see how lonely and sad Abuelita is?

Look, Maya, Abuelita's fine. Not every adult needs someone special.
Our neighbor, Señora Donella, is single and she's not lonely and sad.
Well, that's because she always goes out on dates.

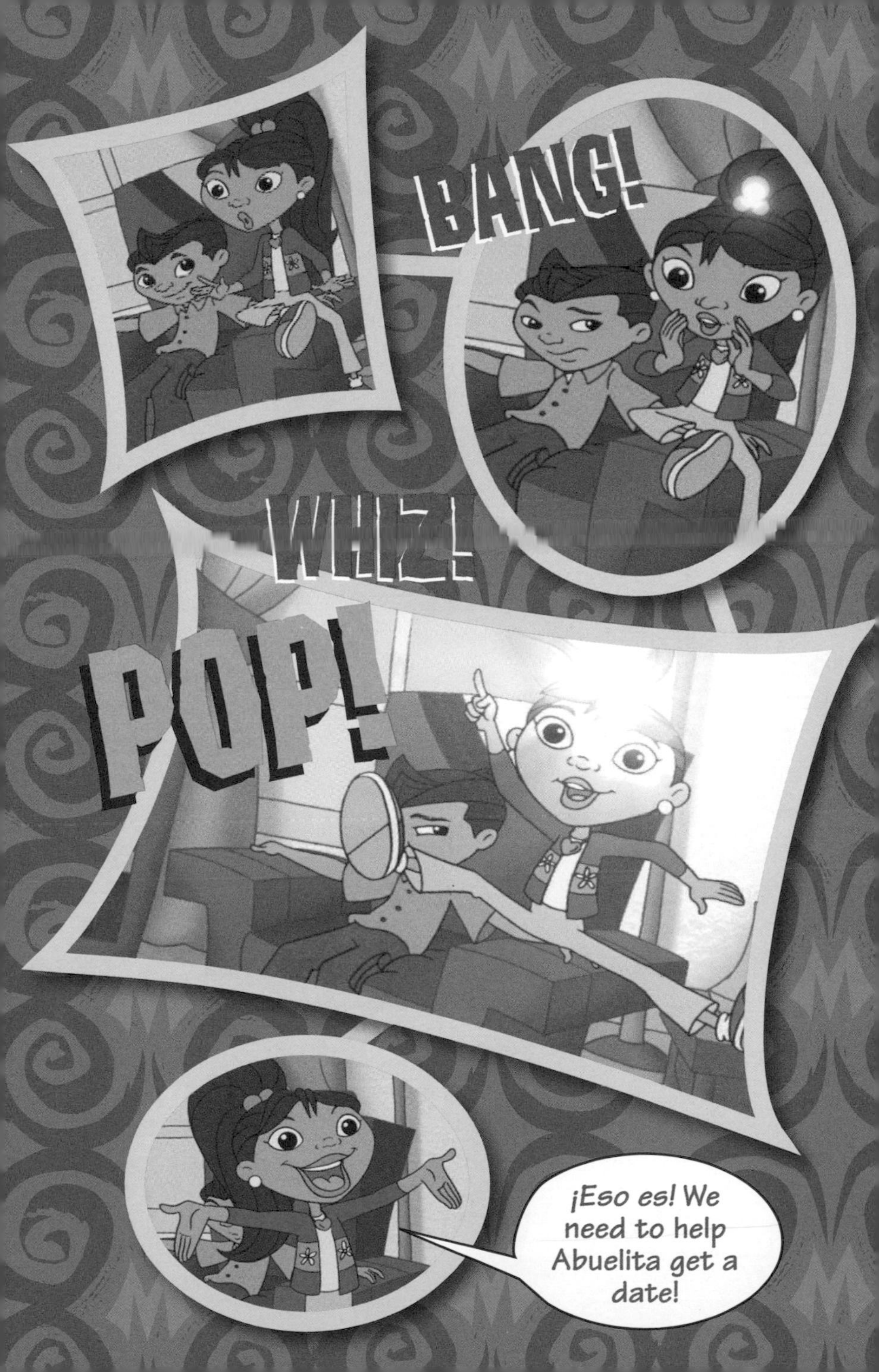
BANG!
WHIZ!
POP!
¡Eso es! We need to help Abuelita get a date!

Time out. Flag on the play.
Don't worry. It'll be fun. I promise.
That's what you said the last time you had a plan. But I ended up pulling cactus needles out of my –
HA HA! Oh, yeah. That was so fun.

Ay, you could never be ugly, *mijita*. Besides, true beauty comes from within.
Gracias, Abuelita. You always know what to say.
Unlike some people.
I'm sorry, Maya.
I know just how you can make it up to me, my twin brother.

Maya, please. Remember what happened last time you tried to help someone get a date?
SQUAWK!
SCREECH!

It's true that Paco was almost eaten by his girlfriend...but I still think they might have worked things out.
¡AY YI YI!
Eagles.

The point is, if Abuela wanted someone, she'd go and find someone herself.
Miguel, she only thinks about others, never about herself.

Maya, no one on the planet but you could think this is a good idea.

Where will you find a date for Abuela?
Of course...I need to go where the eligible bachelors hang out.
Hm, ¿dónde están los solteros?

AND EVEN LATER THAT DAY . . .

Hey! What's going on here?

Move along, please.

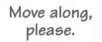

Pase usted, por favor. ¡PASE! ¡PASE! ¡PASE!
They're all too young, too old... or too ick!
At this rate, we'll never find your Abuela a date.
Never say never! I will not rest until my Abuelita isn't lonely anymore.

Hmm...Not unless you were expecting bills. Sorry, Miguelito.
When is my Astropack going to get here already?
Then I can fly around town!
Enough distractions, Miguel... We have to find Abuelita –
– a date...

Buenas tardes, Señora Elena. ¡Qué bonito día!, ¿no?
Buenas tardes, Señor Felipe. It is a beautiful day, yes?
Uh-oh…you've got that gleam in your eye…
There he was, in front of us all this time… ¡El cartero! The perfect date for Abuelita!

PLANS FOR ABUELA ELENA'S DATE TAKE SHAPE IN MIGUEL'S ROOM . . .
I'm just suggesting that we think it over –
Miguel! Please. Less thinking, more doing.
KNOCK! KNOCK!
Hey, Miguel, what are you up to?

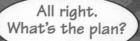

All right. What's the plan?

Well, we need them to show up at the same place at the same time.

Why not right here? Señor Felipe delivers the mail every day...

No, we need someplace more romantic. Algo más romántico...

GASP!

Like the Community Center!

The Community Center? That's the *opposite* of romantic.
Theo, where's your imagination? Think about music, lighting, special effects to transform the place into a romantic paradise!
Andy and Theo...please make the place beautiful. Miguel and I will get them here by six o'clock tomorrow.

Here comes Señor Felipe. You have to slip this package into his bag. Otherwise, the plan will fail.

I'm not sneaking something into Felipe's bag. No way.

Hola, Maya. How are you, Miguel?

Hola, Señor Felipe. Gee, Miguel was just telling me he would like nothing more than to spend the day following you on your route.
Really, Miguel! I would love to have your company.
OK. Well, I have to go. Don't forget about the you-know-what, Miguel.
I'll see you later!

So, Miguel, why is it that you want to spend the day with me on my route?
Er…um…well…the thing is…I'm thinking I might want to be a mailman when I grow up.
¿Pero cómo?
Yes. It seems like such an…um…exciting profession.

You are very perceptive, Miguelito.
Well, I'm about to go back to sort the mail at the post office right now. Would you like to come?
Sure. Uh, sounds great.

BACK AT MAYA AND MIGUEL'S APARTMENT LATER THAT MORNING . . .
Okay, Theo and Andy are fixing up the Community Center, Miguel's got the secret package, and we've got to help Abuelita get ready.
You think she needs our help?
Of course! Her last date was back in Mexico when she was a teenager and had a chaperone.

She needs new clothes, new hair, a whole new look.
You mean...
MAKEOVER!
The thing is, we have to make it a surprise.

BUT SEÑOR FELIPE GRABS THE BAG BEFORE MIGUEL CAN SLIP THE PACKAGE INSIDE . . .

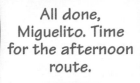

BACK AT ABUELA'S APARTMENT . . .
ZZZZZZZ
My Abuelita's bedroom is over there. Be quiet and follow me.
Stop!
El pollo no. I'll take two pounds of meat instead.
She was just talking in her sleep. C'mon, let's hurry.

PING!

ON THE POSTMAN'S ROUTE THAT AFTERNOON . . .
Stay alert, Miguelito...we are in Toro's neighborhood.
Who's Toro?
GRRR!
GULP

How am I supposed to mix and match? I'm a fashionista, not a magician.
Great. Now what are we going to do?
Okay, think, Maya.
¡Eso es! We'll make a dress.

What are you girls doing here?
Uh, well, see… We're measuring you for a special yet secret dress.
Ay, *mis hijas*. You're so thoughtful. But I have plenty of pretty dresses in my closet.
But we'd like to make you another pretty dress, anyway.
For Chinese New Year!
Because it's the Year of the Dress…

Mm, *bueno*...
You'll need special hair and makeup too.
Yeah. You're going to look so beautiful.
Gracias. But you know true beauty comes from within.
Exactly, Abuelita. Now please lift your arms for me?

Oh, it's just a bird. Well, it's getting late. What's next?
Hmm...I don't remember sorting this package. It's addressed to
"Mi Corazón," at the Community Center? No name, no street...What if this fell into some rookie's hands who didn't know the neighborhood?
Good thing you're delivering it, Señor Felipe. We'd better get it to the Community Center fast.
I see you are a true mailman at heart. ¡Vámonos!

IN ABUELA ELENA'S BEDROOM
EARLY THAT EVENING . . .
Perfecto.
COUGH!
Let me introduce you to the beautiful new Abuela Elena.
¡AY!

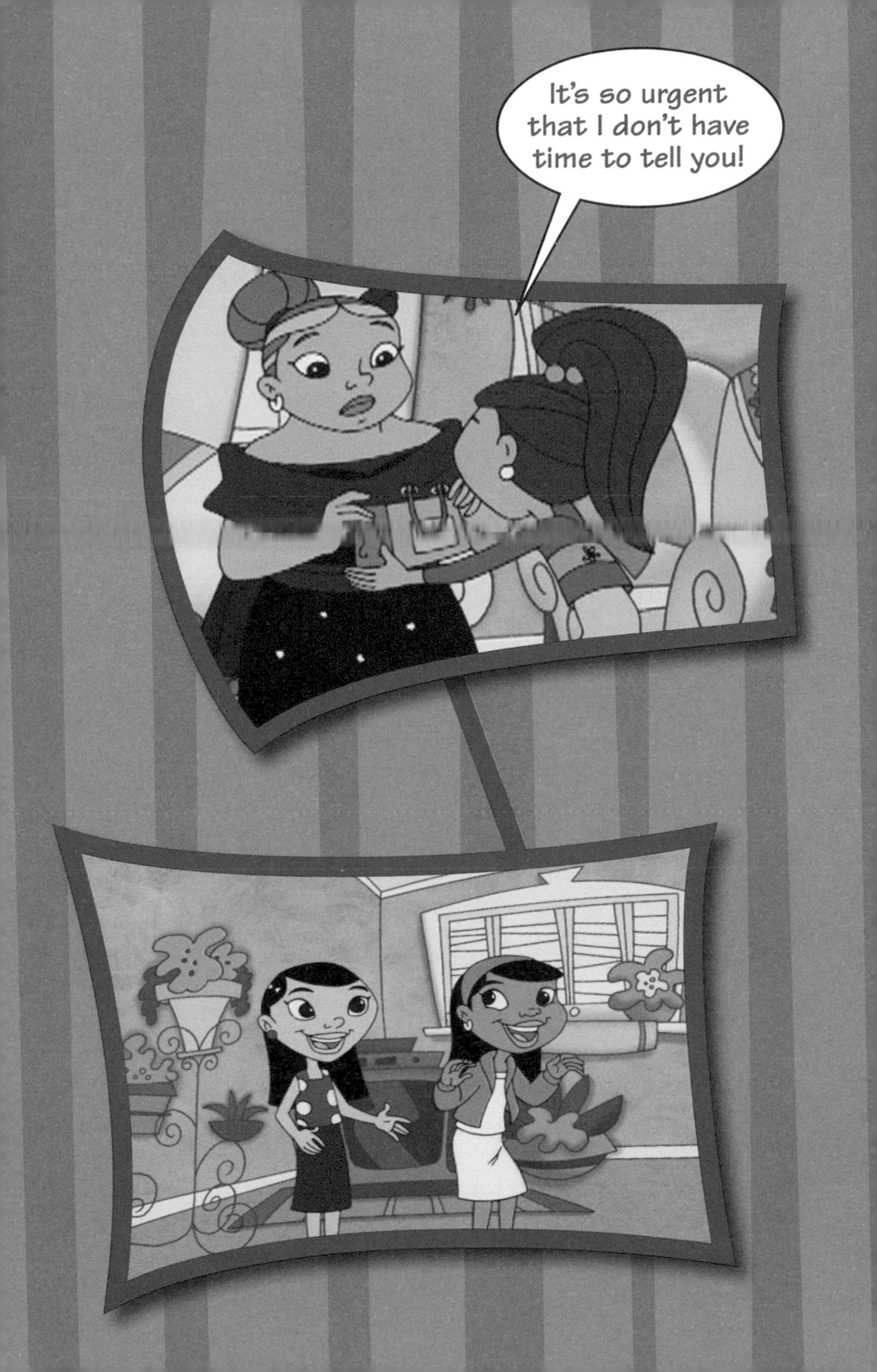
It's so urgent that I don't have time to tell you!

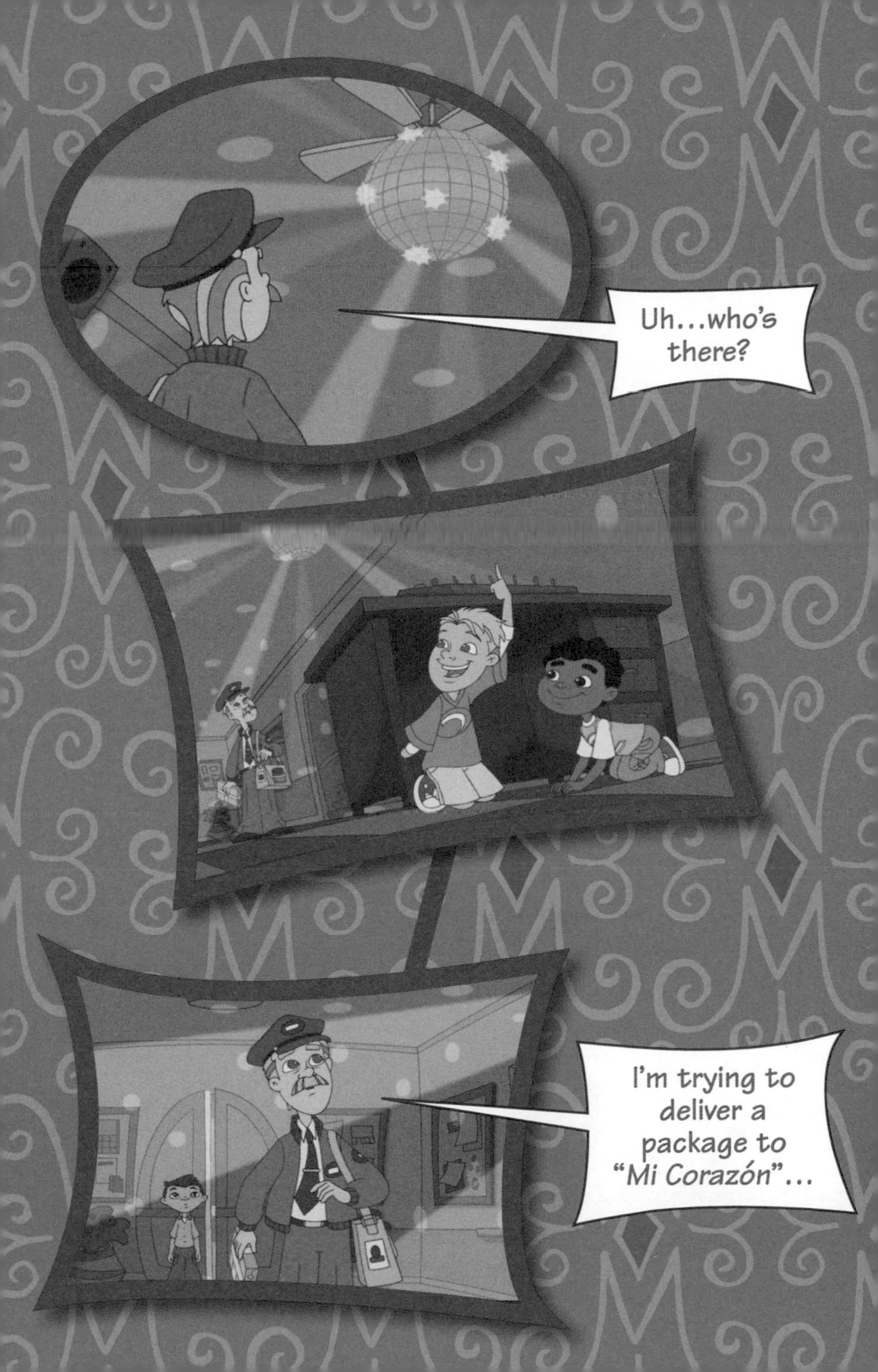
Uh...who's there?
I'm trying to deliver a package to "Mi Corazón"...

"Mi Corazón." How sweet!
¡Ay! Mis chocolates favoritos. I…don't know what to say… Thank you!
Oh, you don't need to thank me… I'm just doing my job. I'm just glad I found you.
Ay, Señor Felipe, ¿gusta chocolates?

...then there's a strange package addressed to "Mi Corazón"...
Miguel...?
UH-OH!
...then I bring the package here, even though it didn't have a zip code, and I find you. Dressed like... well...very nice...So what's going on?
I'm not sure, but I have an idea. ¡Nietos!

What were you trying to do?

Let me start by saying...this wasn't my idea.

He's right.

Mija, I don't understand. Why did you do all this, and dress me like this?

I don't want you to be lonely anymore... You should have someone special. I'm worried about your heart.
My heart? *Mijita, escúchame.* How could I be lonely with such a wonderful family and great friends? I've never felt happier.
And you never have to trick me into taking Señora Elena out on a date. It would be my pleasure.
Really?

Of course. My favorite part of every day is delivering your mail. You have the most amazing smile and beautiful personality.
Maybe that's because true beauty isn't about what's on the outside. True beauty comes from within.
Eso es, mija.

How am I supposed to fly with this? It's just a rubber balloon!
Miguel. What am I going to do with you? Everyone knows that an Astropack needs to be made of titanium.
Tengo una idea...

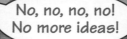

My Astropack might have been a disappointment, but Maya's plan was a success.

Abuela Elena and Señor Felipe have been going dancing every week.

And I learned that being a mailman can be pretty exciting.

But most important, I learned that even though Maya isn't exactly like other sisters... I think that I'll keep her. At least for now.